Hope that you enjoy the book

Mercy of Hades

Millie Bowker

Millie ♡

Trigger Warnings - Blood, Death, Scenes of a sexual nature.

NOT SUITABLE FOR YOUNGER READERS

This is a work of fiction. Names, characters, places and incidents either are the product of the author's imagination or are used fictitiously. Any resemblance to actual persons, living or dead, events or locales is entirely coincidental.

Copyright © 2025 by Millie Bowker

All rights reserved. No part of this book may be reproduced or used in any manner without written permission of the copyright owner except for the use of quotations in a book review.

First paperback edition October 2025

Book cover design by @belladesiree.design
Formatting by Millie Bowker

Paperback ISBN: 9798291862537

Mercy of Hades

For all the girls who watched 'Hercules' and fell for the god of the dead instead of the guy with the muscles.
This one's for you.

We have all heard the stories - Zeus's thunderbolts, Poseidon's wrathful seas, and the might of Hercules.

Tales told as myth, legend, or children's fables.

But what if they were never just stories?

What if the gods of ancient Greece still lived - hidden away from plain sight but woven into the very fabric of the modern world?

Not myths, but powerful, immortal beings - forever watching, protecting and demanding worship from mere mortals.

An exciting thought … until you realise some gods aren't meant to be crossed.

Chapter One

Between Two Worlds
✷
Grace

After a long day of teaching, Grace had finally reached the hospital. Derbyshire Royal Infirmary may as well be a second home to her given the amount of hours she had spent there. Dragging her exhausted body from the driver's side of her tiny Fiat, she slammed the door hard, the piles of marking stacked meticulously in her boot would have to wait until tomorrow. As she approached the towering hospital, the bleeding pink of the setting sun seemed to ooze over the roof. And there, hidden away in the hills, was the misty outline of Olympus - home to the gods - a place no mortal could ever reach.

But what did she care about high and mighty gods with nothing better to do than lounge about on clouds all day?

No, Grace had real problems. And time was running out.

Inside the building, the endlessly long corridors dragged on for what seemed like miles, room after room the same, the stench of clinical bleach burning her nostrils. Following the signs for ICU, Grace hunted for the room labelled 'Fleur Matthews'. Having just turned eighteen, her baby sister had finally made her way off the children's ward to her own private room in intensive care.

Although this wasn't usually the kind of news families would be excited about, a tiny part of Grace's heart was filled with pride. After all, Fleur hadn't hit many milestones in her life, but seeing her become an adult was a miracle.

Even if she was completely dependent on a ventilator to breathe.

The double doors ahead flew open with the push of an automatic button, and Grace dug through her overstuffed handbag in search of a surgical mask - thank goodness Covid was over - but the patients on the ward were so fragile that every precaution was needed to keep them from catching infections.

Something like that could be fatal for Fleur in particular.

Caroline, the nurse in charge, flagged Grace down immediately and looped a reassuring arm around her shoulder.

"We've moved Fleur over to room 301, it's best to have her right in front of the nurse's desk so I can keep an eye on her. You know how her heart gets up to mischief." Caroline beamed as she pointed out the room, a glittering handmade pink sign on the door read 'Fleur'. Grace was forever grateful for the staff that cared for her sister, the time they spent chatting to her or making sure she did not get bed sores meant the world - even though she was entirely oblivious they were there.

Placing her tote bag full of goodies on the bed, Grace leaned over to kiss her sister on the forehead, despite the circumstances she looked remarkably well. Her long blond hair had been neatly braided, the dry skin around her mouth was cleaned and moisturised and the bedsheets were a crisp white. It was so reassuring to see Fleur like this. Grace tried her best to visit every day, however school hours went on far past three o'clock and she was usually up most of the night planning lessons or worrying over SEN referrals.

"Hello you!" Grace said softly as she pulled a few items from her bag, "I brought you some home comforts, seeing as you've got this new room and everything!"

Placing a bottle of rose scented lotion on the sideboard next to their beaten up copy of Pride and Prejudice, Grace smiled to herself, she wasn't sure if her sister could even hear her, but reading together was the best part of the day. Just as she fluffed out the cosy pink blanket on the bed, there was a small knock at the door, almost causing her to jump out of her skin. In all honesty, she had become accustomed to the silence in Fleur's room, it was quite refreshing after spending most of her time surrounded by a gaggle of eight-year-olds.

"Miss Matthews, a pleasure to see you," Dr Williams said as he popped his head around the door, "Mind if I take a seat?"

This couldn't be good. Dr Williams was Fleur's consultant cardiologist and he only ever seemed to appear when the situation was dire. Grace gestured to the hard plastic chair on the other side of the bed, though incredibly uncomfortable, she'd fallen asleep slumped over in one more times than she cared to remember.

"As you know, Fleur's cardiovascular disease has progressed much quicker than we first anticipated. There is now a considerable amount of fluid buildup in her lungs, which is making it difficult for the ventilator to function at full capacity." The doctor leaned over and glanced at Fleur's lips, they had become slightly blue around the edges.

Grace reached out and took Fleur's hand in her own, rubbing a finger slowly across her knuckles.

"I am sorry Miss Matthews ... *Grace* ... there is nothing more we can do for your sister. The best plan going forward would be to consider a new heart, although I'm not certain she would qualify, we always put patients in Fleur's situation on the transplant list if possible - this will buy her some time, but it's not going to be easy," Dr Wiliams spoke with such tenderness. Watching the slow rise and fall of Fleur's chest accompanied by the whirr of the vent.

But the world around Grace seemed to crumble. How long would it take to find a suitable heart? That's even if she makes it on the list in the first place. And if that doesn't work - she is just supposed to be taken off to the underworld?

This is not how it is going to end.

There had to be a way to ensure Fleur had more time, anything to give her a chance at survival.

"Do I need to make a decision right away? I think I need to consider the options," Grace whispered, chewing anxiously at her lip.

"Of course not, I will come back tomorrow and we can discuss further," Dr Williams gave a smile which read, '*Your sister is dying and I don't know what to say.*' before slipping out of the room with a slight click of the door.

Tentatively Grace climbed onto the bed, being extremely cautious not to knock the vent or disrupt any of the monitoring. She simply needed to be close to her sister, she craved the way they used to be snuggled up together as children. In fact, Grace had begged for them to share a bed for as long as possible. The sisters had always been inseparable, and now they lived in entirely different worlds.

What seemed like hours later, Grace shot off the bed in a panic, a blinding white light filled the small hospital room. Hovering next to Fleur's lifeless body was a glowing figure, a stocky-looking man with white wings curled on his back. There was no denying this ethereal sight; it was Hermes.

The time had come. Everyone knew Hermes was responsible for transporting souls to the underworld, but

Fleur was still alive - her heart was beating whether she was controlling it or not.

"You can't do this! You can't take her!" Grace yelled, putting a protective arm out in front of her sister.

Hermes laughed, and adjusted his little cross body bag before pulling out a scroll and studying its contents. The words were written with ink so dark it seemed to burn through the paper.

Holding a shimmering golden hand above Fleur's body and closing his eyes, Hermes declared, "I obey only the Lord of the Dead; if he desires her soul, it is his."

There was no time to waste, and only one choice remained.

"I want to make a deal with Hades!" Grace shouted before the entire room faded to black with a rush of freezing cold air.

There was no going back now.

Chapter Two

The Price of Interference

<u>Grace</u>

Grace hit the ground hard, the breath knocked from her lungs. She sat up dazed and panicking, the silence in the air hung thickly around her. Almost as if the world dared to speak. The glistening ball of light appeared again and Hermes floated to the ground with such ease he didn't even disturb the thick layer of ash beneath his feet.

That's god's for you.

He brushed off the shoulders of his crisp white suit jacket as if this moment was terribly inconvenient for him and gave Grace a look so stern it sent a shiver down her spine.

"I didn't want to do this, you know, Lord Hades hates when I bring living people down here, he says it makes the place look untidy. We much prefer withering souls - you are far too alive for my liking." Hermes grasped her by the arm, dragging her to standing even though her legs shook uncontrollably. She wasn't sure they could hold her up for much longer.

From her new vantage point, Grace could see for what felt like forever down the cave-like corridor ahead, the walls were dark metamorphic slate and seemed to tower above them. A low guttural growl erupted from deep below, freezing Grace to the spot, far too unnatural to come from a dog. It was deliberate, the noise was meant to scare her - and it sounded like something that wanted to be heard.

"Come - we must take you to Hades - he will already know you're here." Hermes set off down the dimly lit corridor, dragging Grace behind him at a pace that was entirely ridiculous for a mortal human. How did Hades know she was here? He couldn't *smell* her, this wasn't some twisted fairytale. And yet, he knew.

This was something more terrible than she could ever imagine. When her impulsivity took the better of her and Grace decided to strike a deal with Hades, she thought she'd simply just have a discussion with the man, preferably in the real world. Under no circumstances did she see herself ending up in the pits of hell.

Moaning noises accompanied their journey to find Hades, voices that seemed to be begging Grace for help. She spun her head around, to see if someone was following them - but the space was empty. She leaned closer to the dripping ebony walls, being careful not to lose her footing on the uneven surface.

'Please, I have done nothing wrong'

'I want to be with my family'

The voices were coming from inside the walls. All of these people trapped in the underworld forever, just because Hades was too selfish to let them rest in peace.

Hermes stopped abruptly, causing Grace to go tumbling into the back of him, but she did not fall against something solid. Instead, his body gave way too easily, soft, yielding and entirely unsettling. Like collapsing against a marshmallow.

The door in front of them was vast, reaching all the way to the matte ash ceiling above. Decadent, glossy wood with a huge golden knocker in the shape of …a skull.

Nothing says 'welcome' like the bones of dead people.

"Are you ready for this?" Hermes spoke, his voice barely above a whisper, his hands shook as he reached out and knocked three times. The boom echoing around them.

There was no reply - but with all the gumption he could muster, Hermes pushed the door open. The throne room was like nothing she had ever seen before, a level of grandeur only acceptable if you are a god.

Carved from black obsidian and glittering clear crystal, the room seemed to glow. The walls reflected the deep crimson flames that burned from the vast fire pit in the centre of the room. Grace lifted her feet and fidgeted on the spot, the floor of volcanic ash seemed to burn through the thin rubber soles of her converse. The jarring bubblegum pink of her usually sensible classroom shoes clashed violently with the grim morbidity of the moment.

A feeling of dread began to grow in her stomach as the unlikely duo made their way to the middle of the room, just inches from the roaring flame that seemed to provide little heat in the morgue-like atmosphere.

Surrounding the room were hundreds of towering glass tubes that reached as far as the eye could see. Grey murky water flowed through them, swirling in a way that almost felt hypnotic, Grace could not wrench her eyes away. At first she thought they may be for decoration, some sick attempt at soft furnishings in the underworld. But as she moved closer, she noticed something swimming around inside, fish?

No bodies.

Or souls rather, grim ghostly faces pressed against the glass, long billowing hair spread throughout the water like seaweed. This was direct transportation to the River

Styx. The tubes vibrated with a humming sound, reminiscent of blood pulsing through veins.

Grace watched as every few seconds a slight flash of light appeared and souls vanished - to somewhere entirely worse. With the distraction of the world's most macabre fish tank, Grace had completely forgotten the reason she was here. Next to her, Hermes cleared his throat anxiously, even other gods were terrified of Hades.

"I have someone here for you, my lord, she wishes to make a deal - it's old magic. Clean, nothing illegal." Hermes chewed at his lip, clearly unsure of the response he would get from the ruthless God of the Dead.

Before them, a figure rose from the vast sculpted throne that sat perched high on a ledge, the perfect vantage point for overseeing the menial beings below. Formed from ebony crystal that shone with a warm light, the reflection of amber gems buried deep within. This wasn't just a *throne*, this was a monument that represented death itself.

Then he was in front of her, just centimetres from her face.

Hades.

There had been no rustle of clothing, no footfall, just a presence that caused a burn of acid to make its way up Grace's throat. She had heard the tales, a god so ruthless he granted mercy to no one without striking a desirable deal in return, a person who haunted the dreams of mortals and thrived on pain. What she was not expecting … was him.

A man standing at least a foot taller than her, with thick broad shoulders and a wide strong jaw. Despite its length and striking black-and-grey streaks, his hair was neatly tied in a bun at the back of his head. And his clothing - Grace had expected a robe, some kind of toga perhaps - but he simply wore a long sleeve shirt that clung to the ripples of his body beneath, form fitting suit trousers followed every curve and muscle of tight thigh. The most surprising thing, however, was his waistcoat, a shimmering copper that complimented the iridescent silver of his skin. She knew he would look impressive, he was a god after all, but this was something else entirely.

And then he spoke.

"Mortals and their bargains," he said, a deep voice filled with sarcasm, "They never seem to read the fine print, but gods help them they are earnest." He began to circle Grace, taking in every centimetre of her, eyes burning a fearsome trail across her skin. "What are you prepared to trade, little teacher? Your soul? A lifetime of crayons and nagging parents for a free pass to the underworld?"

Grace's heart thudded beneath her chest, suddenly her clothes were too tight, her jumper too warm, each hair on her head felt alive. The surrounding air seemed to thin, and he was just *watching* her.

Hades tilted his head, the icy silver of his eyes never leaving her face.

"Well?" he whispered, so close Grace could feel the warmth of his breath against her gelid lips.

"I want to make a deal - anything you want," she managed to croak.

Hades let out a sigh that could cause a landslide and ran his hand across the light stubble on his chin. Grace didn't know what to think; his expression was entirely unreadable. But then his burning gaze fell to Hermes instead, standing as far away as possible and looking entirely sorry for himself. The shimmering white of his wings had dimmed, and they fell limply against his back.

"Hermes, you know how much I *loathe* mortals, remember what happened when you brought Aristotle here? Do I look like the kind of man who enjoys logic and philosophy?" Hades' voice rumbled like distant thunder, it carried the weight of a thousand lost souls. Unsurprisingly, there was no response from the glittering messenger, he just nodded gravely. Grace had no idea what Aristotle had done, but she was going to try her damndest not to make the same mistakes. Hades was not the kind of person you wanted to cross. And currently she was sorely regretting not making a deal with Chloris or Aphrodite - at least they wouldn't tear her head clean from her body.

Hermes was still blithering around and avoiding eye contact. A furious growl burst from Hades, causing the fire pit to intensify, the flames almost licking the ceiling.

Grace shrunk back, attempting to shield herself from the scorching heat.

"Hermes, leave … now," the god commanded, bringing his hand down to his side and letting out a low whistle. Out of nowhere, a wild animal appeared next to him, a panther perhaps? Vast and muscular, every sinew rippling with undeniable strength, almost like a shadow of Hades himself. The animal lunged forward, breathing in heavy ragged pants - his jaw was wide and with each pulse of anger, strings of spittle flew from his mouth, catching in the gloomy light, grotesque and terrifying. Before Grace could even register what was happening, Hermes disappeared from next to her in a puff of creamy smoke.

Fucking hell.

She was alone - with Hades.

What on earth had she let herself in for?

Chapter Three

No Escape from Death

✳

Grace

All eyes were now on Grace. Those of the Lord of the Underworld, and his equally terrifying panther.

It's just a very big cat, you can do this, she thought.

"As I said, I wanted to make a deal. My sister is very sick, but she just needs a little more time! There has to be a chance she can live - and that chance is you," Grace's voice trembled with fear as she spoke, there was no way she was making eye contact, so she just watched her foot making a pattern in the ash.

"Ahh - she speaks," Hades laughed bitterly, his hand finding the soft fur between the panther's ears, earning himself a soulful purr. "Although I'm not certain who told you that I listen to the demands of mortals. I refuse to be manipulated by someone who reads "The Very Hungry Caterpillar" all day. *I am not Zeus.*"

Grace swallowed hard. How did he know what she does every day? Gods were omniscient, but she always presumed Hades had better things to do. Getting him on her side was the only possible way for Fleur to get what she needed - Grace would have to withstand whatever Hades threw at her.

No matter what.

"I am willing to do whatever you say, I just have to save my sister." Pleading with the devil was never going to be easy, so with all the bravery she could muster, Grace looked up. Locking eyes with the very man she feared the most, his gaze a pair of steely grey pools that were haunted by horrors she would never be able to comprehend. The longer he looked at her, the more Hades reached into her soul, pulling out memories that were long hidden and discovering the nightmares buried deep below.

"Now that sounds like permission for me to do my very worst," Hades spat, " But I am a fair man. If you complete three trials of my choosing in five days , I will allow you to return to the mortal world and give your sister more time to get her heart."

Grace's own heart filled with light for the first time since she plummeted into the depths of hell. Three trials - she could do that, right?

"Hades, I..." Grace attempted to give her thanks to the god, but not before she was cut off by a harsh cough.

"I was not finished," he groaned, turning to face the tubes of decaying souls that littered his throne room. "The underworld has a wonderful way of trapping people here ... those who are living will begin to *rot*. My home was not built for anyone with a functioning pulse. You will age rapidly, your bones getting weaker - until you become at my mercy forever. That's if you fail of course ... which you will." Hades laughed again, he was revelling in the idea of her suffering.

"Clearly you do not know as much as you think," Grace whispered under her breath, but Hades never peeled his eyes from hers. It seemed he did not enjoy being insulted.

"Tell me about the trials, then you will see how strong I really am." Grace folded her arms tight across her chest, a sure sign of defiance.

"*Sure*, I always put my trust in puny living women," the sarcastic tone in his voice was infuriating, "For trial number one: you will enter the court and be presented before the Judges of the Dead - Minos, Rhadamanthus and Aeacus. Here you will argue for the worth of your soul - convince them why you are deserving. But be warned... if you tell a lie, even to protect yourself, you will be condemned to Tartarus."

Perfect, nothing like the threat of an abyss of wicked souls to push someone to do your bidding.

"You forget I spend my days surrounded by unruly children - I can deal with more than you think," Grace said, "and I never tell lies."

That wasn't entirely true, she had been called a 'liar liar pants on fire' many times, but what did the opinion of an eight-year-old matter?

"You are awfully confident, but this is only the beginning. Now you will leave me for the night, the rest of your trials will be explained *if* you survive the first one." Hades gestured down to his scary sidekick, "Drakos will escort you to your room - do not leave until you are told. Trust me, that would not be good for you."

Being chaperoned by a killer big cat was something Grace had never anticipated would happen. But as she followed the soft padding of paws, she was strangely comforted by the beast, Hades had called him Drakos - *dragon*. And it was completely clear as to why, for a soft furry creature, he was utterly terrifying to look at, but he stood between her and the writhing mass of souls that clawed at the air, reaching out for help. He remained by her side, a shadowy wall protecting her from the harms of the underworld.

Drakos had orders, and he was going to follow them.

The corridor ahead stretched long and narrow, the darkness of the walls seemed to absorb what little light was being emitted from the flame lamp until they were in near darkness. Strange markings were etched into the ancient stone, some gave off a soft glow and others were so old the surrounding wall was crumbling away.

They stopped at a tall narrow door cut directly into the slate, it swung open by itself only adding to the eerie sensation that hung in the air. Drakos pushed past, entering the room first, his sleek black fur brushing against Grace's leg - she wasn't quite sure when he had decided to be her friend and not tear her apart - but she was grateful for him all the same.

The room was not a cell.

At least that's what she was going to keep reminding herself of. There were no bars or thick steel chains hanging from the walls, just a simple metal chair with a pad too thin to be called a 'cushion'. The torch on the wall flickered, casting shadows that seemed to move independently, and as Grace sank into the chair, Drakos disappeared.

She was alone again, except for the relentless moans that echoed throughout the place.

The almost silence gave Grace's brain room to start overthinking, which was never a good thing.

What if the hospital decided to turn off Fleur's life support without permission? Then she would be brought to the underworld anyway - and everything Grace had endured so far would have been for nothing. But Dr Williams wouldn't do that ... would he?

Alas, that was not the biggest issue right now - the thought of Hades backing out of their deal was a terrifying idea. There was no reason he couldn't kill Fleur anyway, even if Grace did complete the stupid trials, which seemed more and more impossible by the minute. Facing the judges didn't seem too bad, but she knew that each trial would get progressively harder, Hades was not a merciful ruler.

He would make this as hard as possible just for the sheer fun of it.

For the first time in her entire adult life, Grace was doubting herself, she knew she was strong, particularly when it came to problem solving or puzzles. But if any of these tasks required brute strength or imaginable talent, she would be fucked. She knew skipping out on pilates class would come back to haunt her one day - but she never thought this would be the circumstance.

Fighting against death himself.

Chapter Four

The Trial of the Judges
✷
Grace

The door flew open without warning.

Grace had no idea of the time, the lack of daylight in the underworld had entirely wrecked her body clock, but she knew she'd been stuck in that room for hours on end. Sleep had eluded her, naturally, sitting in that ridiculous excuse for a chair hadn't helped. The sweat-damp, rumpled brown knit jumper and leggings, she'd worn since yesterday clung to her covered with a layer of grey dust. She didn't even want to know what her hair looked like, it was tough to tame at the best of times.

There in the doorway stood an ominous figure, one she had become quite familiar with yesterday ... Drakos. He simply waited for her, his thick black tail swishing gently against the ashy floor, bright yellow eyes staring straight at her.

"I suppose you have come to deliver me to my doom?" Grace said as she tentatively stood up, stretching the ache in her back.

There was no need to say anything else, they both knew what was happening; the trial awaited.

Grace's footfall broke the disconcerting silence as she followed Drakos through the hidden maze of corridors, everything seemed entirely different to yesterday. Like the underworld was constantly shifting, always providing a new challenge for its inhabitants. Drakos padded just ahead of her, his huge form like a terrifying sentient shadow. Grace tried not to glance at him too often, but he was simply mesmerising, his inky fur glimmered in the lamplight causing an almost warm hue to emanate from him.

"You don't ... talk do you?" the notion seemed ridiculous, of course, he was a panther! But this was the underworld - home of the Lord of the Dead - if anyone was going to have a talking panther, it was Hades.

The eerie silence continued, Drakos kept his steady pace, not even stopping to look back.

Grace sighed, "Well, I figured that was the case. Of course, I would end up with the strong silent type."

As they turned the corner, the air shifted, it seemed heavier, thicker, almost making it hard to breathe. Grace slowed down, unsure of what was causing the pit of dread to spiral in her stomach. And then, without looking at her, Drakos spoke.

"Keep your breathing steady Grace, they can sense fear," his voice was deep and gravely, filled with the experience of the underworld's demons.

Grace froze, stopping completely. She had to be hearing things, that was the only possible explanation, this place was turning her insane.

"Did you just ... you can *talk*?" Grace was entirely shocked, she blinked at him, trying to regain some part of her sense.

"Yes, when I have to." The words were few, but simply cemented the idea in Grace's brain that Hades sent Drakos to protect her.

That thought was mildly comforting.

At once, the corridor seemed to disappear, spilling out into a vast circular chamber ahead of them. Drakos accompanied her to the threshold, and then stopped, lifting his huge head up and, for the very first time, making eye contact with Grace.

This was it.

"Speak only truth here, lying will end you," he rumbled again before vanishing entirely.

The judgement room was unlike anything in the mortal world. Bright white curved walls topped with a shimmery dome ceiling that was etched with ancient images depicting love, war and death. Scenes of Aphrodite in battle with Ares, sparks flying between the two of them, a deep passion that had burnt for centuries. On the left-hand side was the most ornate image of Hades, his long hair flowing behind him as he surged deep into the underworld, Drakos next to him, as always.

Grace's eyes were soon drawn to the suspended white marble thrones hanging from the decadent ceiling, three of them in total, each one housing a judge of the dead. In the centre was Minos; with his long white beard billowing, the legendary crown of stone upon his head representing the weight of deciding one's fate, and the tangle of thorns covering his eyes ensuring justice was always blind. Grace had heard the stories of Minos, how he had terrorised young children in the chamber of the Minotaur - she knew he would have the deciding vote if it came down to it.

Seated to his right was Rhadamanthus, short silver hair almost clinging to his head, the same colour in his beard. He was a giant of a man, his head towering above the back of his throne, but what made him even more terrifying was the colossal snake coiled around his body. The colour of burnt bronze, its scales reflecting in the sepulchral light as it wound lazily around the neck of its owner, thin forked tongue flicking absently.

Grace could barely peel her eyes away from the serpent when a booming voice filled the room, it was Aeacus. The keeper of the keys of Hades, leaning forward in his throne and setting his fiery gaze upon Grace as she trembled below.

"You must answer our questions with complete honesty; if you lie, we will know. And then there will be no escape - only condemnation to Tartarus." Aeacus watched intently as Grace simply nodded, there was no way she would risk even telling the smallest of white lies.

There was no need, she could do this. She had to do this, to survive.

Aeacus spoke again, this time gesturing for Grace to approach the thrones. The vast pit next to her spat out plumes of milky smoke and with it the voices of regret and sorrow. She tried to block out the wails of desperation - they would not distract her from the task at hand - no matter how much they tugged at her heartstrings.

"If your sister lived, and you died, do you think the world would be better for it?" the god declared, his blood-red eyes never leaving Grace's. The question hit her like a tonne of bricks, she had always wished she could take Fleur's place. But did that mean the world would be better? What about the children at school that needed her - relied on her to nurture them?

"Yes, I believe if Fleur was well she could give more to the world then I ever will be able to," she whispered, "When we were children she talked constantly about her dreams of becoming a conservationist. Specifically red pandas." Grace smiled, remembering all the times that Fleur had poured over pictures of the furry little creatures, showing each and every one to her sister. It had annoyed her a little at the time, but she wished more than anything to spend that time with Fleur again.

"Honestly, I think she is a better person than I am," Grace declared, this was possibly the truest thing she had ever said.

There was no response from the judges.

Grace felt her legs begin to buckle underneath her, she had hoped there would be a hint that she was passing the first trial. But instead, there was just another question.

"Do you truly believe you deserve to return to the mortal world?" it was Rhadamanthus that asked this time, the slithering snake on his arm coiled tight. Grace had pondered this very idea the entire time she had been stuck in the underworld - but facing the truth in front of the very people who were deciding her fate was a completely different matter.

"No, I believe I did the wrong thing. Well, not for me, I love my sister more than anything and I cannot imagine my world without her. But I fear it was a selfish decision." With each word Grace uttered, the snake became looser, less tense, and angry. Almost like her telling the truth was making it happen.

"Fleur is suffering; I think she would have ended her life if given the choice. But I stormed in and made that decision for her."

Rhadamanthus gave a long, slow nod, the first sign of recognition.. Just one more question and then this was over - well the first trial, at least. But the only judge left to speak was Minos, the cruel, coldhearted man who had revelled in sacrificing young lives for his own entertainment. Whatever his question was, it would be the worst of all.

"If Fleur saw you here, would she still love you?" Minos questioned, his voice wasn't loud, it didn't need to be. But each syllable dripped with venom that increased the panic in Grace's chest tenfold. It was almost as if his voice was hypnotising her, trapping her.

"Yes," it was supposed to be a simple answer, sisters always loved each other, but Grace had done something that may have ruined their relationship forever. "But, she would be furious. The fact I have given my life in a rough attempt to save hers, she wouldn't like it. I don't know how long it would take her to forgive me for this - but in my heart I know she will always love me."

The truth lay bitterly on her tongue. In the moment, she had acted on pure impulse, never once considering any other feelings but her own.

Perhaps Fleur would *never* forgive her, and that fate would be much worse than anything she could face in the underworld.

Before her, the three judges sat in stony silence, no movement, no talking, just nothing.

And then they were gone.

The marble thrones swinging empty back and forth, like no one had ever been sitting in them.

The lump in Grace's throat finally broke free, and she began to sob, the quiet echoes filling the hollow chamber. This was the first time she had allowed herself to cry since being trapped down here, but there was simply no holding it in anymore. Her heart ached, and she fell to her knees on the dusty ground, clutching the once soft fabric of her jumper in her hands.

Anything for a little comfort.

"Well, that was *delightfully* traumatic." A cool voice spilt from the doorway.

The only person she did not want to see right now.

Hades.

Chapter Five

Living Among the Dead

<u>Hades</u>

"You -" Grace jerked, fighting to get herself back upright, dragging her limp body from the floor in order to glare at him.

"Yes - me. God of the dead, ruler of souls and apparent babysitter of foolish mortals." He moved closer, his boots scuffing through the ash, causing clouds of grey dust to appear. "They didn't kill you. Congratulations."

"You said they would ask questions … *you never told me* …." She wiped her face with the sleeve of her jumper, a haphazard attempt at rectifying her dishevelled appearance.

With a faint shrug, Hades circled Grace, looking over at the empty thrones. "I said they would judge you. Which they did. Quite successfully, actually."

"I want to go home," Grace gave a whispered beg. But it was no good, Hades was simply enjoying this too much.

"We don't all get what we want, now get up. You have four days left." he spat harshly before vanishing into thin air.

*

Hades found himself retreating to the reassuring solitude of his private room, buried deep within the very heart of the underworld. A place he could escape to, somewhere without the ridiculous prestige of the throne room or the chaos of the River Styx.

The space was relatively small, housing simply his large tourmaline desk, littered with scraps of paper and discarded 'deals' that mortals thought he would be interested in. He had never had much time for the living - when they appeared in the underworld, it was usually at the cost of something they deemed to be precious. But then, they always withered away before completing their end of the bargain.

It was tiresome.

Hundreds of candles sat in neat rows on the mahogany cabinet behind the desk, representing each mortal that had ever dared to visit the underworld. Only one still burned.

Grace was unlike any other human he had encountered, she was infuriating as they all were, but she had an undeniable strength. Hades rolled his shoulders and cracked the ancient bones in his neck, strong muscle flexed and moved beneath the crisp white of his shirt. He didn't need to rest, gods never did, however, his body was screaming at him for something. Like it had a need that was desperate to be fulfilled.

He shook off the ridiculous notion and waved a hand above the burning candle, the flame warped and twisted under his power but eventually showed what he desired, a glowing image of Grace. Hunched over in her chair, whimpering to herself, a pang of ... something ... erupted in Hades' chest.

What on Olympus was he thinking? This was no holiday, the stupid girl had done this to herself. With recklessness disguised by love.

She should not still be here, the underworld ripped through earthly souls like mould ate through bread. Her body should have started weakening by now, she was exhausted, of course, but not quite to the level Hades expected.

With a flick of his wrist, the burnt-out candle next to Grace's roared to life, showing a hazy image of a mortal man from centuries ago. He attempted to trade his life for his wife's but didn't even last the night. Each candle that reignited showed the same thing, these people - *these humans* - never survived.

The idea of the second trial sprang to mind, it seemed almost impossibly cruel, no one had ever encountered Cerberus and returned unscathed. For most, the beast was usually a death sentence.

Eyes tight shut, Hades summoned Grace to his office, telepathy was particularly useful when dealing with stubborn captives.

A wave of milky-white smoke, carrying the rich, almost overwhelming scent of vanilla, enveloped the room as Grace shimmered into existence before Hades, who observed her with a critical eye. Her hair was a soft honey blonde that was cut to brush just against her shoulders. Deep chocolate brown eyes that glinted in the low light, filled with fear, but also a flash of defiance. She looked as though she was built to belong in the mythological world, tall and full figured - unapologetically so, with curves that appeared carved from marble.

And for just a second, Hades hesitated. The Lord of the Dead hesitated, just for a heartbeat, just long enough to take in her striking appearance. He could not remember the last time a mortal had stood before him without crying or cowering, Grace was different.

That was possibly the most captivating thing about her.

"Ah finally," he spat, voice filled with sarcasm, "I thought you might have pulled off a disappearing act, how boring that would have been."

Grace did not reply, the words simply did not come to her, but the look on her face was so scornful she seemed just as fearsome as any of the other horrors lurking in the underworld.

For all of his hatred and contempt, Hades seemed almost fascinated by the mortal, something deep within him caused a gravitational pull towards her. And it was entirely wearing on his immortal patience.

"The second trial awaits you. Cerberus, is no ordinary dog, three heads, all with sharp teeth and tempers that burn like fire. He takes his job very seriously, making sure no one sneaks out - or in." Hades paced slowly, lacing his fingers together behind his back, his gaze never leaving Grace. "Your task is simple enough though, you must remove a single ruby from his collar. Grab it, bring it to me, and you pass this trial."

Grace just stared. Her mouth hanging open and small beads of sweat forming on her forehead.

"I don't quite understand ..." she managed to whisper, "You truly want me to steal jewellery from the collar of a beast so monstrous that every mortal on earth fears him?"

Hades rolled his eyes, the drama was entirely unnecessary - if mortals should fear anything it should be him, not some oversized dog. And anyway, Grace would be quite safe, well ... as long as she did not get caught.

"It's not jewellery," he said, his lip curling in disdain, "It's a protection collar, forged from celestial gold and encrusted with rubies that glow with the power of every soul lost here."

A wave of trepidation came over Grace, leaving her face ashen as she fidgeted with the sleeve of her brown jumper, which was now filled with holes.

"How am I even going to get near him?" she questioned, her voice barely audible.

Hades chuckled, taking a seat and rapping his fingers against the cool crystal of his desk, "That won't be a problem. Surviving the encounter is the real task."

In fear, Grace recoiled from him, her body impacting the wall with a thud as she used it to support her full weight. Her breathing was rapid, chest rising and falling in a panic. Hades had rumbled her - he was finally getting the upper hand - or so he thought.

"I will survive," she murmured, "I know you want me dead, but I will survive. I have to."

"If I wanted you dead, you already would be." Venom dripped from Hades as he leant across his desk, "But I want to see how you react when death isn't just a threat, it is standing right before you."

Grace swallowed hard and then nodded.

Hades raised a silver eyebrow, that was an unexpected response ... but so be it.

Let the hound have his fun, let her attempt to prove him wrong.

At least it would be fun to watch.

Chapter Six

The Trial of Cerberus's Chain
*
Grace

The vast room seemed to echo around Grace as she stood in stony silence, tendrils of pearly smoke curled around her. She tucked the sleeves of her jumper over her hands and blew a warm breath into them, the icy cold was bone chilling. Her next trial had begun, and this one seemed even worse than the first.

From the depths at the back of the chamber came a deep growl, the vibrations rattling around her, causing ash to crumble from the walls. A gigantic form moved amongst the mist, the body of a beast, three gargantuan heads swinging from side to side.

Cerberus.

Having escaped the sheer cover of his hiding place, Grace could see the mythological animal in his full form. Slick black fur covered every inch of him with an oily shine.

A pair of blood-red eyes set their sights on its prey - much to Grace's dismay, the prey appeared to be *her*.

She noticed the chain hanging from Cerberus's neck almost immediately, a thick golden loop that appeared forged by the gods (*obviously*) with a group of rubies hanging from the centre. There was no way she could reach it, the three-headed dog towered far above her, leaving the prize she so desperately longed for entirely inaccessible.

The walls in the chamber were made from thick matte basalt, jagged shards protruding wildly from its surface. Almost like ... *steps*. Grace clambered over to the wall, ensuring to duck from the cascade of drool making its way from the beastly jaws above her.

She took hold of the first piece of rock form, dragging herself against its rough surface until her feet were firmly bedded. The climb was not going to be easy, but there was simply no other way to do this. As she reached up to the jutting layer of volcanic matter, her jumper snagged against the surface, causing her to falter slightly. The sharpness cut through the thin fabric like butter, leaving the pale skin of her forearms exposed.

Continuing her ascent, Grace clutched the small pieces of crumbling stone, her knuckles turning white under the pressure, but if she fell, there would be no saving her.

No return to the mortal world, to Fleur or to her normal life.

Beads of cherry red blood began to appear on her arms as she battled higher, looking over her shoulder Grace could see Cerberus's giant nose twitching as he caught hold of her smell in the freezing air. She had to hurry up, or she was definitely going to end up as lunch.

Sizing up the gap between her shivering body and the giant beast, Grace decided her best option would be to attempt the treacherous jump and grasp hold of the collar, wrenching the ruby from its encasement before Cerberus had time to grab her. Inching slightly further up the incline, she wiped at the blood that was now oozing from the deep cuts on her arms and readied herself for the terrifying leap.

Feet firmly on the rock ledge, she looked once more at her target, snarling ferociously, plumes forming in the air from the heat of his breath.

This was it.

Summoning every fibre of strength in her exhausted body, Grace leapt from the rugged wall, flying across what seemed like miles of icy air before landing on a warm, sturdy surface. She had made it, well ... she had made it to his back.

Crawling forward tentatively, she reached out for the chain, her fingers wrapping around the cool metal, but as they reached the very edge of the first ruby, the body beneath her began to shake.

An ear splitting yowl travelled throughout the empty chamber. Attempting to grasp hold of any fur she could find, Grace slid from the body of the beast, her scream disappearing into the air as she plummeted into the abyss.

Her back hit the floor first, a piercing pain spreading from her hip all the way to her shoulder, but that was the least of her problems. Six sets of fearsome eyes towered above her as droplets of spittle landed in huge puddles on the ground.

A paw the size of a planet loomed, taking a swipe across the easy prey that lay on the floor in front of him. Jagged claws made contact with delicate skin almost immediately, ripping a deep gash across the tenderness of Grace's chest. She screamed in pain, her hands trying to reach the incision and stop the blood that was now spilling freely from the wound.

Never in her life did she anticipate this would be her death … and then there was a voice. Cold, harsh, and rough, cutting straight through the room.

"Paúō!" Hades yelled, appearing next to Grace, his silvery skin glittering in the low light. He held out a hand in front of Cerberus, the force of his presence causing the creature to lower his massive heads and retreat into the smoke with the yelp of a puppy.

Kneeling beside the body of his bleeding mortal, Hades took the navy handkerchief from his pocket and pressed it lightly against her chest. A bolt of sheer electricity pulsed throughout Grace's body as his hand made contact with the soft pink of her skin. Hundreds of images flashed through her brain in an instant, almost as if the contact with the god of the dead had created a sort of innate connection.

"You need to get up," Hades demanded, grasping Grace by the arm and attempting to steady her on her feet, "This cut needs tending to, and you are bleeding all over my floor. It is such a menace to clean."

Even in times of crisis, the bitter, sarcastic tone never left Hades' voice, he held Grace against the side of his body and she shivered, pulling herself away. But the blood was now gushing from the cut, and the feeling of lightheadedness was encapsulating her.

"Just stay still, I will transport us to my room to get this sorted. If you stop fidgeting around, that is," Hades hissed.

His room? She had no business gallivanting around in the bedroom of the most menacing god on earth - no, she would be fine. Maybe just a sit down and a glass of water would do the trick.

After attempting to move again, Grace's knees buckled beneath her and without the support of Hades, she definitely would have collapsed like a badly stacked deck of cards.

Perhaps she did need help - he was only going to tend to her wounds - what was the worst that could happen?

Chapter Seven

Something like Mercy

✻

Grace

Grace had never expected to see Hades' bedroom, let alone allow herself to be led inside while clinging to life. But still, it was nothing like she had expected. Although she didn't have much experience with ethereal decor, there were no ostentatious golden fabrics or marble pillars - it was just dark, stony and silent.

Rather like its occupant.

The walls stretched high into an arched ceiling filled with the amber carvings of a thousand stars, giving a pulsing glow. Dark wood encrusted with obsidian crystal housed the bed, grey-washed linens were neatly tucked in at the corners and the comforter looked plush and warm - exactly what Grace needed. Cool air circled the room, carrying the faint scent of smoke and rainwater. To the left lay a burning fire casting its light upon the tall shelves, littered with a myriad of books, scrolls and potion bottles with labels Grace couldn't understand.

But there were no mirrors, no ornaments, not a single hint of self indulgence. Just crisp, clean refinement.

And yet on the bedside table sat a plant, a small sort of succulent in a black pot. Not living but not dead either, almost as if it was clinging to life.

Why would the mighty Hades, lord of the underworld, be caring for a plant? And for a moment, Grace couldn't decide whether this room was built to keep people out or to keep a secret in.

"Come. Sit." Hades spoke curtly as he took her by the shoulders and seated her on the bed, the luxurious mattress giving way as her body melted into the comfort she had so missed.

"I am fine," she whispered, attempting to claw together the remnants of her jumper to cover the exposed skin of her décolletage. But the shreds of fabric were doing nothing to hide her modesty, and the blood that was now drying clung to her white bra.

"Yes - you seem fine. Everyone fairs well after a battle with Cerberus." Hades said as he sifted through the bottles on his shelf, casting aside Nepenthe and Vitae until he reached the bulbous brown glass bottle hidden in the back. With his hands covered in Grace's blood, he lifted the bottle to his mouth, securing the cork between his teeth and pulling hard.

Grace retreated on the bed, lifting her hands to protect herself, "What is that? I do not want anything from you - you might kill me for all I know!"

Hades chuckled as he swirled the midnight blue liquid in the bottle.

"I have told you already, if I wanted you dead ... you would be." Reaching out and tearing away what was left of her jumper, Hades caused a shriek to emanate from his mortal charge.

With her breasts exposed, Grace felt more at risk than ever, but the look in the gods' eyes was not one of lust, more so of worry. He took in the full view of her wound, three long cuts running from her left collarbone and across her chest, ending just under the top of her bra. It did not appear life threatening, but still it hurt like a fucking bitch. Hades caught her eye briefly before returning his attention to the bottle in his hand.

"Just stay still - this will be painful - but only momentarily. You have to trust me, can you do that mortal?" his voice was barely above a whisper as he angled the bottle ready to pour the mysterious liquid.

Grace nodded and clenched her jaw tight.

Dark fluid spilled onto her chest with a fiery burn that she felt to her bones, but it was only for a second. The angry red edges of the skin began to move and pulsate, they slowly drew inwards, beginning to knit together. Torn skin was repaired, bruises fading and the usual paleness of her chest returned.

She could not believe her eyes, it was magic. Humans didn't heal this way, if they did, Fleur would have a chance at survival.

This was simply the work of the gods.

"I have never seen anything like that in my life," she whispered, running her hands over the perfect skin.

Hades averted his gaze at once, working diligently to return the cork to its rightful place, and keeping his eyes as far away from Grace's breasts as possible.

"Yes, well, I can't imagine they have Kykeon in Derbyshire. But it seems to have done the job." he said, replacing the bottle on the shelf. "You need something to wear, I can not have you strutting around the underworld in a state of undress."

Grace nodded, "Do you have anything? And by the way, *I don't strut*."

A throaty chuckle came from Hades' throat catching her entirely by surprise, she did not know he could laugh -

63

not a real one anyway - usually they were only used to taunt her.

Tossing her a creamy colour shirt from his wide black wardrobe, he turned to face her, "Take this, I will leave you to change. You may rest here until I return, Kykeon is good - but only if you allow yourself to heal. And you need to be ready to face your final trial." His mouth curled into a smile, but it was false, never meeting his eyes. For a split second Grace didn't see the man who had tended to her wounds, but the ruthless god of the dead.

Hades slipped from the room, leaving her alone once again and at once Grace felt a new sense of self-preservation. Lingering in his bedroom left her more vulnerable than ever, she needed to find her way back to her own room. And to Drakos, he would protect her, or so she hoped.

Grace gathered the shirt around her, sliding her arms into the silky sleeves, wincing slightly as the fabric made contact with the small cuts and grazes. She did each button up one by one with shaky hands before rolling the sleeves to her elbows.

Standing on unbalanced legs, she took in a deep breath of cold air before blowing it slowly out of her nose.

Pull yourself together, you have to survive.

As she made her way silently towards the door, Grace eyed up every bottle of mysterious potion on the shelf, each turned over book or torn piece of paper. These things belonged in the underworld, they belonged to Hades. Running her fingers lightly over the shelves as she passed, an immense sensation of warmth filled her body, like she was being taken over by the sun, but as soon as it came, it went. And the icy chill returned once again.

Something about making contact with the god of the dead, or even touching his belongings, made Grace feel uneasy, like it gave him power over her mind and body.

But that was wildly unacceptable.

She was a woman determined on returning to her sister and nothing, not even a strong, *some would say handsome* god would stop her.

Chapter Eight

A Voice Wrapped in Rhyme

<u>Grace</u>

The hallways seemed different. In fact, everything seemed different. As Grace made her way from Hades' room tucked deep within the underworld, she felt utterly confused. Walls that had once blocked the way had disappeared, but new off-shoots and pathways had emerged from the smoke. The ashy floor beneath her feet rocked unsettlingly, the movement making her queasy.

What was happening? This place was changing by the second - almost as if the underworld was purposely trying to disorient its inhabitants.

Grace stopped for a moment, running her hands through her hair and taking a deep breath, she needed to get back to her room. But the passageway seemed to be sapping the very energy from her body as she moved.

Losing her balance slightly, her foot slipped from the edge of the path, a cascade of stones falling into the abyss below. Then came the hands, cream ghostly fingers wrapping around the bright pink of her shoe, crawling up her calf, causing an icy sensation to trickle down her spine. Fear crept over her like a cloak, encapsulating her in its clutches. Wrenching her leg from the power of the souls, Grace fell back onto the floor, her already aching bones clattering against the harsh terrain.

That was all it took.

More and more appeared, wailing and whispering - poking at her ribs, dragging her arms to force her to join them.

"Stop! Get off me - I am not one of you!" she screamed, kicking hard, her foot colliding with ghostly space instead of an actual body.

She was terrified.

A fierce wind blew - and then a figure appeared.

It seemed so real this time, not a soul or a vision ... a deity.

Standing just before her with a glittering lilac arm held in the air, the souls retreated into the chasm, screeching as though they were being tortured. Finally free from their inhumane grasp, Grace flew to her feet, hunched over; she wretched, burning acid filling her throat.

"Thank you," she managed to utter, "They would have killed me if it were not for you."

The figure just stared at her.

Grace was unsure who the ominous figure was. Their presence felt different from anyone else she had encountered in the underworld - hazy and mysterious.

Her skin shimmering in what little light emanated from the lamp hanging from the ceiling, it rippled faintly, giving her an ethereal glow. Deep violet eyes, darkened by sorrow and time, studied Grace slowly, almost as if she could read her future.

Curls of jet black hair streaked with indigo fell down her back, tight ringlets that sat perfectly. She wore no crown or armour, just a woven wrap clinging to her form, the rich plum colour accentuating the pastel tones of her skin.

There was a stillness to her, almost as if she were a statue - and then she spoke.

"You wander far, you mortal flame, lost in halls that shift with shame. The path you seek won't stay for long, not when your heart beats so wrong,"

Grace startled, the rhyme the woman spoke made little sense.

"I ... who are you?" Grace asked, watching the woman with great interest.

"I am Megara, a Furie true, I see the secrets that cling to you. Your questions burn and your fear runs deep, but answers from me do not come cheap." Megara spoke, her voice like silk.

Well, the rhyming thing seemed to be a trend, Grace thought. As if the underworld wasn't confusing enough, this woman ... *this Furie* ... seemed to make the whole situation worse.

Megara circled her slowly, a wry smile on her lips, "The King once bled for love so bold, but now he turns all warmth to cold,"

Grace attempted to speak, but a single glittering finger silenced her.

"His garden weeps though none can see, what pain it is to set love free," Megara finished, looking rather satisfied with herself.

"I don't understand," Grace pleaded, "What king? Do you mean Hades? Does he wish to harm me?"

There was no response.

Just an eerie silence hanging between them.

With a rush of glacial air, Megara disappeared.

Leaving the hallway empty once again.

Grace faltered for a moment, that was possibly the oddest conversation she had ever had. If she could even classify it as a conversation, it was rather one sided - and *rhythmic.*

Surely the king Megara had mentioned was Hades? Turning warmth to cold sounded rather like him, although she had also mentioned love, and that was something he seemed unable to feel.

The Hades she knew was fierce, bitter and sarcastic to the core - who had he loved? And more importantly, who had loved him in return?

Ahead, the hallway seemed to have righted itself, the towering grey walls unmoving, and the floor steady once again. Grace made her way back to her room, pace quickened slightly, she was not interested in encountering anymore deadly souls, or Furies for that matter.

Drakos lay in front of the door, his giant form lolling on the ash, eyes trained on her.

"You would not believe the day I have had," she said, attempting to step over the great cat tentatively, "No, you stay there, I'll manage."

The panther did not seem to care about her woes, or the fact that he was rather in the way, but his presence had become quite comforting. And Grace wanted him there because she knew as soon as Hades discovered her missing, all kinds of anger were going to be unleashed on her.

Hopefully, Drakos would prove a good body guard.

But there was one thing she needed to do before Hades appeared. Kneeling on the basalt floor, Grace swept her finger through the dust, writing carefully.

'The king once bled for love so bold, but now he turns all warmth to cold. His garden weeps though none can see what pain it is to set love free.'

She was determined to remember every word of that poem, and no matter what - she was going to discover its true meaning. The underworld had already taken enough from her, and with each passing minute her heart ached to be home again; to spend hours in the hospital with Fleur, to plan lessons and go to staff meetings, anything for her life to return to normal.

Grace chewed at her lip, the anxiety of the final trial loomed like a storm cloud, although her injuries were now healed, she still worried that they would cause a setback. She had no time for inconveniences, she had to survive whatever Hades threw at her. Even if it nearly killed her. The lord of the dead was not going to make things easy for her, he hadn't so far anyway, all he had done was confuse her.

His diligent act of kindness still stood out in Grace's mind - the way he had tended to her cuts, the softness in his eyes replacing the usual fury. Nothing made any sense, he was supposed to hate her, to be punishing her. But in that moment there was another feeling in the air, a tension that was palpable.

A feeling Grace craved to experience again.

Chapter Nine

Divine Feminine

<u>Hades</u>

Hades was enraged.

How dare this menial mortal disobey his direct order? It wasn't hard really; she simply had to stay put in his room until he returned, but no. Instead, she was off gallivanting around the underworld, getting herself into all kinds of danger. He knew the furies would find her before long, those meddling women couldn't help but get themselves involved in the drama.

That was all he needed.

For Grace to find out about his history, to see a 'soft' side to him, it had been bad enough that she had recognised his worry over her injuries. She did not need to know he had been a man who had *loved*, but had lost the only person that brought light to his life.

Persephone was his secret. To the outside world, she had simply got involved with the wrong man, given her life to be with Hades, that's what her mother had thought, anyway. But what no one saw was the genuine love, the hours spent together simply just existing. And then she was torn away from him, not physically but mentally, so she would never love again.

It was all happening again now that *she* was here. Grace was the only woman since Persephone not to shrivel under his icy gaze, not to beg and plead with him for compassion. No, she was strong, infuriatingly so. But it filled him with fascination, which had to stop immediately.

The third trial was approaching rapidly, and this was going to be the final straw, there was no way someone with such a strong moral compass could survive it. Grace would wither under the pressure, and then she would be stuck in the pits of the underworld forever.

Which is exactly what Hades had wanted *originally* — for her to be at his mercy, to taunt and scare her. Now all he wanted was for her to be as far away from him as godly possible.

Everything about her set him on edge; the way her ashy hair fell in front of her face when she was concentrating, the delicate curve of her hip, the wry smile that appeared whenever she challenged him. It was all too much, this could not happen again. He simply wouldn't allow it.

When Grace lost the final trial, he would send her to the Asphodel Meadows; plain, boring and incredibly dull. The place Hades dispatched the most tedious of souls to, there she could not reach him, to entice him with her feminine strength and power. It was the only thing that would remove the overwhelming ache in his chest, a feeling he had been unable to dispel ever since he had laid eyes on her for the first time.

Hades fell back onto his bed, unleashing a deep groan as he did so, the ceiling above him shimmered with a smattering of stars, and he watched as they flickered and changed. *What was going on?* He was overcome with emotion like some lovesick teenager, this was not how the ruler of one of the most terrifying places on earth acted, it was almost embarrassing really.

"What would you think of me?" He spoke aloud to no one, turning onto his side and coming face to face with the plant that lived on his bedside table. *Carpobrotus.*

That's what Persephone had called it, Hades chuckled slightly, it meant Ice Plant - fit for a man with a soul glacial as the bitter chill that blew through the underworld.

"I failed you," he whispered, not that the plant could answer, the conversation was more aimed at the woman who gave it to him. Someone he had not seen in a very long time, "I will not let it happen again, I promise."

The final stage of Grace's ordeal had to come soon, Hades decided. For he could not exist around her a moment longer, or he would simply burst into flames.

Chapter Ten

The Garden of Persephone

<u>Grace</u>

Painfully cold air blew under the door of Grace's room as she sat huddled on the chair, blowing some warmth into her freezing hands. All night she had pondered over the poem Megara had told her of a king who had once loved, and still it made little sense. But this room was proving more and more claustrophobic by the second, she had to leave - to find a way out - before something more sinister happened. And it was going to, Grace could simply sense it.

The illusory corridors seemed to be on her side this morning, as she followed the twists and turns deeper into the heart of the underworld. She wasn't entirely sure what she was even looking for, a window or door perhaps, but no that would be too easy. Hades would have made sure escape was impossible, she had experienced his security system already, and she was not eager to come face to face with Cerberus again.

Whispering wails echoed off the slate walls as Grace battled with the thickness of the air, rooms she had never seen before appeared and then vanished as quickly as they came. Shaking the floor and sending a cacophony of stones cascading from the ceiling. Ducking and avoiding any near-death experiences, Grace backed into a passageway she did not recognise.

An intoxicating floral scent encapsulated her immediately; roses, lilies and wild daisies unfurled their perfume in waves so dense it felt almost smothering. The aroma was cloying and seemed to cling to Grace's nose, but deep down there was a feeling of relief. This was the first sign of life she had encountered since entering the underworld.

Silence filled the space, and Grace moved carefully, each step sinking into the dense soil; there wasn't a clear path through the undergrowth, just trampled down leaves creating a winding route, and at once the garden began to appear around her.

It was beautiful.

Not in the same way the living world was, it was different, ethereal somehow. The flowers were familiar - narcissus, foxgloves, marigolds - but the colour seemed drained, as if someone had pulled the very life from them, leaving behind a shell.

Once blush-pink roses had faded to antique ivory, violets had lost their usual purple hue. Even the greenery was mossy and tired. She reached out, trembling fingers brushing the edge of a lily petal, it withered beneath her touch as if it recognised something within her.

This garden wasn't dead - it was trying, struggling to stay alive.

Every plant seemed to be reaching towards some unseen light, clinging to survival in a place that knew no mercy. The thick perfume was heavy with a sweetness that almost turned bitter if she dared to breathe too deeply.

No birds. No wind. Just whispering petals.

Grace took a pause in the centre of the garden, overwhelmed by the sheer weight of it all, this wasn't a place for her. It felt almost sacred, like trespassing into someone's heart. But who had built it? And why was it hidden down here, beneath the world of the living?

She followed the sound before she saw it: a soft trickle, the rush of something flowing just beneath the surface. The garden opened into a small clearing, a narrow stream curled around the edges, the surface like glass. Nestled in the far corner was a structure, part shelter, part throne carved from pearlescent stone veined with dusky pink. Vines wound their way around its columns, ivy tendrils blooming with unknown flowers.

There, seated in its heart, was a woman.

Grace hesitated. Her breath caught, unbidden.

This was no mortal woman, she emanated a soft rosy glow, her skin shimmering like frost in the moonlight. Deep chocolate brown waves of curly hair spilt over her shoulders, and her eyes - when they met Grace's - were both kind but ancient.

She didn't rise from her perch, there was no need, the woman commanded respect with her mere presence.

"Grace," she said, "I have been waiting for you."

The words, although spoken gently, caused Grace to falter slightly, her heart stuttering in her chest. She felt exposed beneath the woman's gaze, as if every thought she'd carried was quietly unfolding in her wake.

"Who are you?" Grace asked, her voice barely above a whisper.

Tilting her head, the woman gazed upon the mirrored pool, a ghost of a smile on her lips, "I am Persephone, Goddess of Spring."

The name settled like a shadow.

Persephone.

She had heard it before, the goddess was legendary. A girl taken by the god of the dead, forced beneath the earth and made queen against her will. It was a cautionary tale of a tragic figure, some spoke of her entrapment in golden chains, others swore she ruled as an equal.

But no one really knew the truth, other than Persephone, of course.

The stillness of the garden felt eerie, as if frozen in time around them.

"They say I was stolen," Persephone murmured, fingers trailing through the nearby blossom, "That I wept for the sun and withered in the shadows."

Silently, Grace just listened. Every story she had ever heard echoed those same words.

"That is not what happened," Persephone explained, "I fell in love; with the underworld, with its peace ... with the man who ruled it."

Grace almost scoffed, "With Hades?!"

Just hearing his name seemed to dull the glow of the goddess, but she nodded slightly, "He did not take me. I came here willingly, I loved him. Perhaps a little too much ...

that was my mistake, I suppose. My hubris did not impress the gods."

"You were punished?" Grace asked, brown eyebrows furrowed.

Lifting her gaze to meet the mortal, Persephone continued, "Nemesis does not take well to overconfidence. Love is sacred, but I was wrong in thinking I could keep it forever, and that angered her." She shook her head as if recalling a bitter memory, "I was cursed to never love again. Not truly. The feeling arises occasionally but will not take root."

A feeling of sadness bloomed between them.

"What about Hades?" Grace dared to ask, her voice hushed.

"He loved me still. Even when I could not love him in return. This garden was built for me, a place I could feel alive even when I didn't want to. He visited often at first, we sat in silence and enjoyed each other's company. But time … it changes things, even for gods."

Grace's chest tightened, a sensation of sympathy and something else she couldn't explain.

"How long has it been?" she questioned, not sure of what to say.

Persephone smiled, but it didn't quite reach her eyes, "A long while, or maybe not long at all. It is hard to tell down here." She gestured to the smooth marble bench next to her, and Grace obeyed, settling tentatively by the great goddess.

"He's not what you expected, is he?" she asked, her eyes moving over Hades' shirt clinging to every curve of Grace's body.

"He is cold and distant." Glad to finally express her true feelings, Grace raked her hand through her hair and sighed, "Like he doesn't want to be touched by anything."

"That's because he doesn't. Not anymore," the goddess told her, "There was a time when he was softer - not the same way as you mortals - but he cared. And he loved me."

Hades' dark, unreadable eyes came to mind - the way he had watched Grace as if she was a prize he could not claim.

"You surprised him mortal, he won't show it, not in ways you understand. But he's watching, remembering what it feels like to *want* something."

"Why me?" Grace responded, her stomach filled with butterflies.

"I do not know, child. But there is a new thread being made by the Fates, I can sense it," Persephone spoke, "This third trial will test you in ways you could never imagine. Hades desires you, but he does not trust you. That is what he wants you to prove. When the time comes, you must follow your heart."

With the finality of her words, the goddess returned to her hidden shadows. There was nothing else to say except, "Thank you," Grace whispered.

And then she stepped away, following the path out of the garden, the scent of lilies and earth trailing behind her like the last breath of spring.

The third trial awaited.

This time it was not about survival - but truth.

Chapter Eleven

The Uneasy Truce

<u>Grace</u>

After emerging from the decadent garden filled with life and hope, Grace returned to the usual dim gloominess of the underworld's hallways. Contorting and pulsing as if they breathed beneath her feet, she made her way down the narrowing paths. In her hand, she clutched the blossom of a rose, wilting and withering in the heat of her palm, a fading reminder of the beauty she had witnessed.

Uneasy silence echoed around her, broken only by the tread of her shoes in the grey ash. Persephone had opened her eyes to ideas she could have never imagined - that Hades could love, and he had done, until his heart was broken through no fault of his own. He was so hurt by the loss of his true love that he had turned into a bitter man devoid of any genuine emotion.

It all seemed unfathomable. But deep down, Grace knew Persephone was telling the truth, and she promised herself she would share the goddess's *actual* story with the world.

Looming at the end of the hall was an instantly recognisable figure, tall with lean muscles, a cascade of dark hair streaked with silver tied loosely in a bun.

Hades.

Instantly a bubble of panic arose in Grace's stomach; this was the first time she had faced him since her rather impromptu escape from his bedchamber, and from the thunderous look on his well-chiselled face, he was not happy.

The iciness of his greyish blue gaze seemed to bore into her soul, to bring forth every fear or negative feeling she had ever experienced. He didn't ask her where she had been, it was obvious he already knew, but when his eyes fell upon the shrivelled petals in her hand, his shoulders sank slightly.

"You disappeared," Hades stated, "I told you to stay in my room, to wait. But clearly you disobey everything I say to you." His shoulders were tight with anger and a balled up fist lay by his side.

"I didn't realise it was a command, more a suggestion," Grace fired back, shrugging slightly.

"Everything here runs on my schedule, I do not make *suggestions* on how you should spend your time," His voice was deep and gravelly, his glare never leaving her body, "I see you have visited the garden."

"Is that a problem?" Grace retorted an eyebrow raised, eager to see his reaction.

"No. I am merely curious to hear what she told you," he answered, unshaken by her retaliation.

"Only that the third trial would be nothing like the others, and that I should prepare myself," she said before lowering her voice slightly, "among other things…"

"If you think that knowledge will help you, you are mistaken," he replied, dark eyebrows lifted slightly.

Grace scoffed, "If you think I scare that easily, *you* are the one who is mistaken." She pointed at him and regretted it instantly, for the look on his face was thunderous.

"Perhaps," Hades added, "most people wouldn't still be here - but you are."

"Is that your way of admitting I have surprised you?" Titling her head slightly, Grace watched for any signs of Hades opening up to her, instead he simply shook his head and continued down the corridor.

"Come. You must get back to your room. It is not safe to wander around."

Attempting to follow his quick pace, Grace stumbled after him, their bodies almost touching as the narrowness of the space grew tighter, more claustrophobic. She could feel the heat radiating from him, the sheer sensation of power and strength.

With all her focus on the vastness of the man beside her, Grace did not notice the uneven ground beneath her feet. The rubber at the front of her shoe snagged on a rock, and she went hurtling forward at an alarming speed.

A hand flew out, stopping her from falling, strong fingers wrapping around the soft flesh of her forearm. Bolts of what could only be described as electricity surged throughout her veins, and for a moment her heart seemed to stop.

"Are you okay?" Hades asked, faltering slightly before letting her go. He seemed almost unsettled by the reaction to the touch of their skin, as if it was a sensation he had never experienced before.

"I ... I'm fine," she responded before brushing the stray hairs from her face and allowing herself to catch her breath.

What the fuck was that? She wanted to ask, but from the uneasy look on Hades' face, he wasn't so sure himself.

Coming to a stop outside of her room, Grace dared to look at Hades a final time, they had not spoken for the remainder of the walk, simply continuing on in silence.

"You've proven... more capable than I expected," Hades began, "but you need to be aware that fall you had back there - it wasn't just an accident - it is a sign that the underworld is weakening your body, claiming you as its own."

"Careful, that almost sounded like a compliment," Being sure to *ignore* the second part of his statement, Grace leant against the slate wall. She had recognised undeniable changes herself already - the way her bones ached, her hair was coarse and tough, every step she made seemed to take more energy. But she wasn't going to let Hades know that, for him to see her as feeble.

"I am not your enemy, you know," she added, "You seem hell bent on making me yours though - mind the pun."

"Perhaps not," Hades replied, "This final trial will be a test of inner strength, it is not something you can fight through."

"Sounds rather personal," Grace said, watching as Hades simply nodded.

"It is."

Their eyes met, and for the very first time it didn't feel like a contest, like a battle of wills where no one was the winner. This time there was a vague feeling of mutual respect.

"I must leave you. I have work to do, souls to condemn ... you know how it is," Hades explained with a stiff sort of smile, "Rest."

Grace followed his figure as he moved once again into the darkness, the grey smoke and freezing air seemed to swallow him up. She retreated into her room, falling almost at once to the ground, her back against the wall she drew her knees up. Her trousers were more holes than fabric, the garish pink of her shoes dulled by layers of volcanic ash, the shirt that clung to her body was slick with sweat but still gave her an odd comfort. Hades had given her this, the man who ruled the dead, who turned lives upside down and relished doing so.

None of it made any sense.

And more than anything, why did she crave to be near him? To experience the pull of her soul, to touch him, explore him.

She was supposed to hate him.

But that feeling seemed to be fading by the second.

Chapter Twelve

Trial of the Obol

✷

Grace

Morning came fast, not that Grace had slept anyway, but it seemed like mere minutes since she had parted with Hades at her door. Now she was sitting anxiously in her chair, foot tapping against the floor, fingers fidgeting with the edge of her shirt.

Beneath her clothing, her muscles ached and her bones screamed for rest, but it would all be over soon. Today was the last trial.

And she was going to be ready to face it.

A surge of warm air filled the room, and Grace quickly realised she was being teleported - Hades' favourite way to get her exactly where he needed her.

Before she could even come to understand what was happening, she fell to the ground with a thud. But this was not her room, not anymore in fact, she had never seen this place before.

Cut like a scar through the landscape was a river, wide but winding, water black as oil. Distant wails and sobs carried on the light wind, blades of deep dark foliage blew slightly, drops of damp water clinging to their edges.

"Grace, welcome to the River Styx," a voice spoke before Hades appeared from behind a rather ominous looking tree, his shimmering silver waistcoat making his skin appear even more ethereal than usual.

He gestured to a hooded figure standing on the bank, a long ferryman's pole clutched in his skeletal hand. There was only one person this could be, Charon, carrier of souls and general guardian of the river. Towering above both Grace and Hades, he watched over them with fearsome burning red eyes, his gnarled fingers tapping on the side of his pole.

"This is Charon," Hades explained. "He is usually responsible for ferrying souls to the ... nicer ... part of the underworld. Those that can pay give him an obol coin to earn passage - those that can't, well they are claimed by the river forever."

Grace edged forward and looked tentatively into the water. Mangled bodies twisted and writhed together, faded faces contorted in agony. It was like nothing she had ever seen before. A terrifying way to spend eternity, an existence no one would ever want.

"What am I doing here?" She demanded to know, averting her eyes from the macabre sight.

Flipping a rather large golden coin over in his fingers, Hades watched her closely, "Today you will be somewhat of an assistant to Charon. I have two souls who both can not pay his fee - but with this coin you can decide to save one of them. To give them a life of pleasure in the underworld, but whoever remains will be destined for perpetuity trapped in the ever-changing waters of the Styx."

Grace could not believe what she was hearing.

The eternal fate of two completely innocent people was going to be in her hands? The pressure of deciding someone's future, dead or not, was too much to deal with.

"You can not give the coin to both. You can not keep it for yourself. You have to choose, that is your trial." Hades spoke once more, dropping the golden obol into her hand, his eyes never leaving her. As if he were expecting some kind of protest or response.

But no, Grace understood the weight of the moment.

The coin was warm beneath her fingers and seemed to hum with magical energy. With a wave of his gaunt hand, Charon summoned two souls from the water.

A woman at least seventy years of age, with a head of curly silver hair. She was hunched over but tried her best to make eye contact with Grace, giving her a feeble smile.

And a man, a boy really, not much older than Fleur. Tall and lean, he had clearly been a sports player when he was alive, he looked so healthy. When he caught Grace's eye, he gave a sort of halfhearted nod before returning to staring at his shoes.

They seemed so *real*. Except for the fact that their creamy skin was glowing, the edges of their bodies hazy. These people had been alive, they had families that missed them, and now their fate was entirely in Grace's hands.

Cold air seemed to choke her as she looked upon the poor souls. A damp metallic stench made its way up her nose, and it took everything in her not to wretch. The noise of the constant churning river water was relentless, a forceful sound that filled her brain.

"I need to know more ... I cannot make a decision like this," Grace said, "Tell me about yourselves."

The woman spoke first.

"I am ready," she spoke softly, "I have lived a full life; loved and lost. I have made my peace with death ... but the Styx... it terrifies me. It is no place for an ending, I simply want to rest."

Grace understood that completely, even being in this part of the underworld was sucking the very energy from her body. And she was alive, she could leave this place, but one of these people would be trapped here forever.

Because of her.

Stepping forward, fists clenched at his sides, the boy began to tell his story, "My life hasn't even begun, I just started my first job, I have parents, friends … I shouldn't even be here! I can't be lost to the water, I deserve peace because my life was stolen from me."

Again, Grace was filled with a rush of empathy, of course, the man deserved the coin, he had died so young. Why shouldn't he get a peaceful ending? But then surely the older woman, who had lived a long life, deserved a restful eternity?

Grace's fingers twitched around the obol, it was throbbing in her hand, itching to be released.

"Tell me," she asked the woman, "if I gave you the coin, would you truly feel at peace?"

"Yes, I believe so," the older woman replied, "I have no more to give to life, and it has no more to take from me. My only fear is the cold of that water... pulling me down..." The woman stopped and steadied herself, she looked so scared.

Grace turned to the boy, "If you had lived, what would you have given to the world?"

The boy almost laughed, "I had big plans," he said, "I wanted to be a scientist - I recently started my first postgraduate job before ... well you know. I have never been stupid or reckless, and yet here I am. If I end up in the Styx, any good I have done won't matter, anyway."

From the corner of her eye, Grace could see Hades watching - not the souls - but her. His expression was unreadable, but his eyes trained on her face.

The two souls before her waited, the obol glinted in her hand. Her mind span, mercy or fairness? Both feared the Styx, both deserved peace - but she could not save them.

Persephone's words played over and over again
"When the time comes, follow your heart."

She had to decide to go with what felt right, it didn't matter what Hades or Charon thought, this was her decision. And she had to carry that around for the rest of her life.

Her fingers traced the very edge of the coin, moving over each tiny indentation, gaze falling upon the older woman's face, Grace took a deep breath and held out the obol.

"You deserve your rest," she declared.

The woman simply bowed her head, a wash of relief coming over her as she pressed the coin into Charon's hand and boarded the ferry.

When they disappeared into the mist, the boy's breathing became ragged, "I thought - I thought you might understand!"

Grace swallowed hard, "I'm sorry, I…"

Before she could continue, the river stirred, black hands, little more than bone wrapped in sinew rose from the surface, clutching at his legs. The boy screamed, kicking, but water surged up like a living beast, engulfing him in waves of icy water. His skin began to blister, then slough away in strips of ragged flesh as the Styx claimed him entirely.

Cries faded to bubbling gasps as the river dragged him under, leaving only ripples and the stench of burning.

Grace was frozen to the spot.

Her stomach churned, and she fought down the bile that climbed in her throat. The sounds of the boys' screams still ringing in her ears.

Hades' voice broke through the sound, "The Styx takes what it is given."

"You made me do that. To kill him." Grace spat, fury in her eyes.

"No, he was already dead. You simply decided where he would end up." Hades corrected her, not even giving the river a second glance.

"I did it - I completed your stupid trials. Can I go home now?" The thought of returning to Fleur was the only thing keeping her going, every second of the day she longed to be with her.

"I decide when you leave here, Grace, do you understand?" His voice was deep and filled with an unknown emotion.

"But you..." she tried to reason with him, she had fulfilled his requirements, why was he so determined to keep her in the underworld?

"I said, do you *understand*?" Darkness oozed from Hades, who now stood mere centimetres from Grace, his breath warm against her gelid skin.

A single tear rolled down her face.

"I hate you," she whispered.

"There is a very fine line between love and hate." Hades said bitterly, "Perhaps you need to decide on which side of the line you stand."

Smoke curled into a fine mist as Hades disappeared, his last words hanging in the air like a curse. Grace stared into the black water, numb, the memory of drowning screams etched into her brain.

She had no idea where she stood - only that she wanted the world and its relentless choices to stop.

Forever.

Chapter Thirteen

The Weeping Grove

<u>Grace</u>

The trees were crying, and the underworld was listening.

Following her rather traumatic morning at the River Styx, Grace found herself wandering once again through the underworld. This time she followed no route or bothered to take heed of which direction she was heading in - she simply just walked.

Towering overhead was a canopy of black trees, white sap dripping down their trunks like tears. *What was this place?* It was somewhere she certainly didn't recognise. Nestled between the huge tree roots were pools of inky black water, the smooth surface reflecting the lifeless sky above, accompanied by the sound of trickling water that drew her deeper into the glade.

Occasionally, whispers travelled through the space, the voices of those who had been lost to the underworld and were trapped in purgatory forever. Bright white tree resin caught Grace's eye, and she reached out a shaking hand, fingers brushing against the cool smooth wood. It seemed to hum with life beneath her palm, causing cascades of shimmery liquid to spill freely from the branches. The glistening surface showed Grace an image she was trying her best to forget, the screaming face of the boy she had sacrificed, the skeletal hands grasping at his flesh.

The whispers in the air seemed to amplify: the boy's voice calling her name, pleading for help, blaming her for his demise.

Grace covered her ears, but the sound was inside her head now, penetrating her skull and poisoning her mind.

He's gone because of me. But I chose the right person, didn't I?

The surrounding grove seemed to disagree. Dripping in the distance grew louder by the second, each drop mirroring the thudding of her heartbeat. But she could still see him, even when she closed her eyes tight, as vivid as the moment it had happened.

Stop. I had to choose. It was the fairest way.

More whispers - they were turning into shouts now and Grace clenched her hands tighter against her head, the sound of her throbbing pulse echoing. The trees seemed to lean closer, trapping her with their unforgiving darkness and overwhelming presence.

I can't do this, she thought, *I can't carry this with me and survive whatever comes next.*

Vast pools spilt across the landscape, and without a second thought, Grace raced to the edge, falling on her knees before the water. Her breathing was coming fast and ragged as she stared into the abyss - if she disappeared here, no one would ever find her.

Not that anyone would care about looking for her anymore, not after what she had done.

She was still being suffocated by her own thoughts when the sound came; not the continuous drip of tree resin or the faint wail of souls, this was a fierce and relentless roar. Instinctively, Grace turned towards it, growing louder the deeper she ventured into the grove, she pushed through the pale barked trees until they gave way into a narrow clearing.

With the air around her becoming sharp and pungent, Grace saw a huge black waterfall cascading into a turbulent river, the water's rhythmic motion almost hypnotic. She didn't need to be told where she was anymore - This was the Cocytus, the River of Wailing.

She was about to step closer when movement caught her attention; four figures standing near the edge of the waterfall. The first was tall and robed in fabric that moved like mist, a vast pair of creamy feathered wings were tucked neatly at his back. This had to be Thanatos, controller of peaceful transitions in the underworld.

Beside him stood three women, one of whom was easily identified as Megara; the Furie who spoke only in rhymes. The other two must be her sisters, thankfully their backs were turned, there was no time for poetry today.

Shrinking back against the trees and running her hands through her hair, Grace's stomach dropped, the haze blurred her view, but the group's voices remained clear.

"The mortal walks straight and tall, yet down the road she'll trip and fall," hissed one of the women, lip curled into a sneer.

Megara tilted her head and regarded the waterfall intently before speaking, "A softened king will lose his crown if he allows such a woman to drag him down."

So the topic of conversation was her and Hades *yet again*. Perhaps it was to be expected, seeing as the underworld had received no new gossip in the last thirty lifetimes.

Thanatos's voice was deeper and more calm, "He is not ruined, not yet. But you ladies should be careful. This mortal may not break like all the rest."

Grace's breath caught, then came the pull - the strange magnetic string between her and Hades - he could feel it too, she knew it. But the thought was soon veiled with doubt, if he felt something, *anything*, towards her, why did he not speak to her? What was the fun in letting her suffer this way?

His words at the Styx came to mind: *There is a fine line between love and hate*. Wasn't that the truth.

Turning his head slightly, Thanatos stiffened, his gaze didn't quite meet hers, but it seemed he almost sensed her presence.

"Enough," he murmured to the Furies, "Don't you have any work to do?"

They dispersed into the mist without another word, their bodies absorbed by the darkness, the roar of the waterfall seemed even louder in their absence.

Grace stayed hidden in the shadows until the murk in the forest began to clear, but even then she felt it - that pull towards Hades, fierce and unwanted, coiling tighter with each step she took in the opposite direction.

Chapter Fourteen

Amber in the Obsidian

✱

<u>Hades</u>

Dust motes hung lazily in the air as Hades sat slumped over in his vast armchair, Drakos slumbered peacefully on the floor next to him. Papers and discarded deals were scattered on the desk, and the final flickering candle behind him began to fade. The day had been long; seeing Grace in such distress at the River Styx had been almost painful to witness, the way she watched as the young boy had melted into the water, eyes filled with regret and fear. And what had Hades done to help?

Nothing.

Except spout some rubbish about love and hate. What did he know of love, really? The only woman he had ever cared for had been brutally ripped away from him, and in that moment the god of the dead had sworn never to let another woman rule his heart.

That was until Grace appeared, all curves and chocolate eyes - the vision of her standing in his throne room for the first time was one he would never forget. She was terrified but gave not one hint of weakness, she still hadn't, in fact, her confidence was rather unwavering.

All the trials she had faced, the sheer cruelty Hades had shown her, anything to make her break, to falter under the pressure of the underworld. But even when she failed for the first time, when Cerberus had his way with her, cutting flesh from bone, Hades stepped in and saved her. That was *not* supposed to happen, he was planning on letting the beast end her like he had done to so many other captives in the past, but hearing Grace in pain struck him right in the heart, like glass shattering in his chest.

The feeling had simply been instinct, an unavoidable draw towards this mortal woman, it was like nothing he had ever experienced before.

Hades groaned aloud, "How did this happen to me, Drakos? I cannot simply let her leave. Go back to her boring life in the mortal world; she is more than that, much more, she is as worthy as a goddess in my eyes. Athena or Artemis could not demand more respect from me."

The lounging panther looked up at his owner, thick dark tail swishing against the plush carpet rhythmically.

"You have to follow your ... well, your heart, Master." Drakos spoke deeply, he very rarely shared his opinions unless entirely necessary.

"God, you sound like you have been talking to Persephone," Hades mocked, "that is something she would say." Chuckling slightly, he reached a shimmering silver hand down, caressing the soft fur between the panthers ears, "I know Grace has visited her, although how she found the garden in the first place I will never know. What must she think of me? A man happy to leave his love to wither away in some garden buried deep in the pits of hell."

A rumbling purr from his companion gave Hades the will to continue.

"I swore this would not happen, but when I look at Grace, it is ... *different*. She makes me feel like I could be more than just the lord of the underworld, more than a man scared of his past and terrified for his future. She reminds me what it feels like to care without fear, to love without resolve."

Drakos shifted, and the king's hand found itself buried in a mass of sleek inky fur.

"You have to tell her about the girl though, Master, of the sister she leaves behind. If you truly love her, she must know the truth."

Hades knew his animal confidant was right, Fleur was struggling in the mortal world, any day now she would fade between the lines of living and dead. He had to be the one to tell her, he would not allow her to see her sister appear in the underworld without warning, it would not be fair on either of them.

"I will tell her when I see her next," he murmured, "I hope then she will see the man beneath the darkness, because for once I want to be someone she can trust; someone who can love her for eternity. Literally."

Hades knew he had no right to demand love from Grace, not after the misery and pain he had put her through, but the yearning in his heart was undeniable, and she felt it too - he had seen it in her eyes.

If Grace wanted war, he would give it to her. But if she wanted him.... Well, that would be far more dangerous.

Chapter Fifteen

Fire and Ice

✱

Grace

Hours of aimless walking, had delivered Grace to the courtyard. A gloomy mix of shadowed corners and bright marble arches that reflected the silver of the underworld's false moon. Grace didn't even know how she'd ended up there in the first place, she had simply followed the ache in her chest like a hound on a scent - sharp, throbbing and nearly unbearable. It had led her down hallways, pulled her through doors ... but then there he was.

Hades leaned against a blackened pillar, arms folded across his broad chest, narrow grey eyes glinting in the low light. It was as if he had been waiting for her.

"This," she declared, jabbing a finger against her sternum, "it hurts. Every second, every hour I am away from you, it gets worse but I feel the ache dissipating with each footstep as I near you."

A slow smirk rounded his mouth, "It hurts, does it?" his voice was low, "So you can feel it too?"

"Feel what?" Grace demanded, her breath had caught in her throat, but she refused to give him the satisfaction of seeing her falter.

Hades' gaze was fixed on her, "The pull. The bond. Call it what you will ... but it's fate."

Grace laughed a short, sharp scoff, "Fate? You're telling me some sort of invisible thread has decided we're what ... bound together? It's ridiculous, I don't believe you."

Something flickered in his eyes - heat, frustration, hunger. "Grace," he said slowly, as if her name was delicate on his lips, "I do not *believe* we are bound, I know it. The Fates themselves have declared it."

Her chest felt as though it was on fire but filled with ice at the same time, "If this," she gestured to the small space between them, "is fate, then I want nothing to do with it."

Hades' boyish smirk vanished almost instantly, and he closed the gap between them with a single stride. "You think I wanted this? After everything I have been through, you think I wanted to be shackled to someone who could never love me?"

She should've stepped back, distanced herself from his encapsulating presence, but she didn't, "Then perhaps we should both agree to sever this thread."

Her heart pounded so hard it physically hurt.

Hades hand shot out, fingers curling around her wrist - not with malice, yet firm and unyielding, "If it were that simple I would have done it the moment I laid eyes on you," his voice dropped drastically, it was deep and barely above a whisper, "But the truth is Grace, I can't, and neither can you."

Oh, how she hated him for being right.

But she hated herself more for wanting him anyway.

Hades' eyes roamed over her entire body, lingering slightly too long on the curve of her hip and the softness of her breasts, "You can give me every fiery response, every glare, every ounce of mortal angst. But it will not change what you are to me."

Grace felt herself trembling under his gaze, "And what is that?" she whispered.

"Mine."

The word ignited a passion within her, like a spark to dry kindling. She wanted to push him away, then she wanted to pull him closer, heat coiled in her stomach and tension filled the air as the night seemed to hold its breath.

But she did nothing. Because, god help her, she wanted to see how far he would go.

He didn't kiss her - not yet. Instead, his thumb grazed her cheek, the heat lingering long after his touch had passed. The pads of his fingers trailed down her throat, pausing at the hollow where her pulse thudded strong enough to betray her.

His gaze remained locked with hers, as if this was another one of his trials, one she did not want to lose. When he finally closed the last inch between them, the kiss came all at once - no soft build up, no hesitation - just pure fire breaking through stone.

Hades' hands found her with a possessive strength, one gripping her hip, the other sliding lower to follow the curve of her bum, pulling her tighter against him. She fell into the kiss, her own hands having found their way to the hard planes of his chest, powerful muscles moving beneath the black fabric.

The kiss was heat and ruin, surrender and defiance, it felt like falling and flying at the same time. She didn't know who moved first, who surrendered second. All she knew was that nothing about her world - above or below - would ever be the same again.

Hades' lips left hers, but his hand remained at her waist, holding her like he couldn't let go. The burning fire in his eyes had dimmed, leaving behind a glow Grace didn't quite recognise. But she had a feeling the mood was about to change.

"I have to tell you something," he began, "Your sister's time has come. No healer in your world or mine could bring change to that now. I want to spare you the agony of seeing her suffer."

Grace shook her head, this could not be happening - she had fulfilled every trial, battled every demon - just for Fleur to die anyway? It was cruel. "You don't know her ... you cannot be sure of this!"

His grip on her waist tightened, not in cruelty, but in certainty, "I am sure. Her body can not survive much longer. But I promise you this: when her soul comes to me, she will not wander lost or broken. She will see only the gentlest passage, the kind reserved for royalty. Fleur will want for nothing in my realm."

She thought she had imagined it at first, the kindliness in his tone, the hesitation as he spoke the truth to her. But no, the man before her - the one who had haunted her, tested her - was different now. His glittering silver eyes were no longer cut through her like blades, they carried something different, a warmth ... a longing.

And she did not know how to react.

In Hades, she had seen only cruelty, the fire and rage that flew from him. But tenderness? That was something she had not prepared for.

His thumb lingered on her left cheek, as if he dared to move away, "Grace, is there anything left for you in the mortal world? Anything that calls you home?"

The question struck her hard. She opened her mouth, shut it, and then swallowed down the burn of sadness that ached in her throat. Fleur's name hung on her lips, but she knew what awaited her baby sister.

As much as it had hurt, Hades had spoken the truth - painful and brutal - but the truth, nonetheless. And if he cared enough to spare her from suffering, that had to mean something?

Didn't it?

Chapter Sixteen

Eternal Life

Grace

What felt like hours had actually been a few seconds. And Hades watched intently as Grace chewed at her lip, she had to give him an answer, standing there gawping like a fool was not going to be helpful - even if telling him the truth would be the hardest thing she had ever done.

"It was Fleur," she began, "She was the reason I have fought to return home, why I refused to give up. But now ... she is gone. And when I look at you - when you touch me - I never want to be apart from you."

Hades' breath faltered, like her confession of love had ground everything he knew to a stop. For a moment, the Lord of the Underworld looked almost undone. His hand slipped from her cheek, following the shape of her throat and down across her collarbone. Pale creamy skin exposed at the top of the shirt she wore - his shirt - that still comforted her in ways she would never be able to explain.

"If you wish to stay here," he said, voice low and steady, "you will not survive as you are ... if you wish to be mine for eternity - you must become immortal."

The ache in Grace's chest doubled. She wanted him, oh gods how she wanted him. She craved his touch, his promise of protection, the way his lips had claimed hers.

But eternity was ... well, forever.

The word coiled through her brain. Eternity meant never seeing the sun, meant giving up the job she had worked so hard to achieve, to never live in the mortal world again.

Her voice began to tremble as she finally found the words, "I want this, Hades. I want you. But forever is ..." She hesitated, searching his face for reassurance, "Forever is a heavy vow."

Hades did not waver, not for a second. He stepped closer, the air between them changing from the electric passion that had sparked their kiss to something softer - slow and deliberate. His fingers brushed hers, an action so delicate she nearly missed it.

"Forever is the only vow I can offer you," he explained, "But know this, if you stay here it will be as a ruler, my equal. A Queen."

The words seemed to sink into her soul. Queen of the Underworld. It all sounded so perfect, so achingly beautiful.

Until she recalled Persephone, alone in her garden, basking in her memories and unable to make new ones. It did not seem right to take the place that should have been hers.

Grace summoned every scrap of confidence in her body, "Then it must be done tonight. I must become immortal."

Hades' brow lifted, a flicker of surprising joy altering his usual composure.

"But," she added, holding her gaze on him steady, "Persephone must give her blessing. I will not take her throne whilst she is buried in the shadows of a curse. I will not do this without allowing her to share her voice first."

For a moment, there was silence. His jaw flexed, pride and reluctance flashing across his face, yet beneath it there was something else. Respect.

"If that is what you wish," he agreed.

*

Thousands of blossoms drooped under the pale glow of the garden, the petals echoed the vibrant colours that used to be. Grace understood this place now, a world of sanctuary for a woman who deserved more. Beside her, Hades walked like a man cast in chains, his usual broad shoulders were tight, and his face gloomy. She could practically feel the tension in the air, the way his presence disrupted the equilibrium of the garden.

Persephone was seated once again in her marble arbour, the softness of her rosy glow illuminating the area. When she lifted her gaze, she immediately beamed.

"My girl," she said, "you have returned to visit me."

Grace managed a small smile, "I have. But I am not alone this time."

The goddess's eyes drifted past her, landing on Hades' heavy frame tucked partly in the shadows.

"Hades," she whispered, although there was no hatred in her tone, no pent up emotions, the name seemed hard for her to say.

"Persephone," Hades responded, giving her a short bow.

For a heartbeat, everything stood still.

"It has been a long time since you have visited me here," Persephone declared wistfully, "I thought you had forgotten about the garden - about me."

Hades' jaw ticked, and for a moment Grace feared he may retreat behind the cruel mask he was so used to. Instead his voice came quietly, "I could never forget you. But I thought it was kinder to stay away. To see you trapped under Nemesis's curse when you had lived so freely beside me - I could not bear it. I thought my absence would spare us both pain - and for that I am sorry."

Persephone rose slowly from her seat and, for the very first time, Grace saw her not as a goddess, but as a woman. Weary of the world, but grateful to hear words she had forever longed for.

"And yet I have lived in pain for all of these years," she told him, "but now you give me the apology I have always wanted. What has changed you?"

Her eyes flew immediately to Grace, who stiffened under her gaze, but something in her chest told her to stand her ground.

"It's you ... you have softened him," the goddess marvelled, "You have melted the ice that surrounds his heart. I never thought I would see it happen."

Grace's throat tightened, "I did not mean to make him change. He terrifies me - he infuriates me - but I cannot ignore the pull in my heart. It is stronger than fear, stronger than reason."

Persephone gentled, she almost smiled, but when her eyes met Hades's she became serious "Do not allow this one to fall to tricks of the Underworld, do not let her wither away."

The tension in the garden was palpable, but Grace stuck to the plan. Persephone's opinion was important to her, "That is why I am here," she began. "Hades has asked me to stay, to be with him for eternity. But I cannot - I will not - do anything without your blessing. I refuse to take your place without it."

For the first time, something cracked in the goddess's composure. Her usual rosy hue burnt deep magenta, and she reached out a shimmering hand, brushing the coolness of her fingers across Grace's cheek.

"You speak with all the confidence of a goddess," Persephone admired, "and I can already see the eternal bond growing between the two of you. It is not my right to deny you my child, but if you so wish - you have my blessing."

Grace took Persephone's hand in hers with a squeeze, "And you have my vow, I will tell your true story. It will always live on within me."

"Then go!" the goddess exclaimed, "Eternity may be a long time - but you will want to get started as soon as possible, I am sure!"

As the couple walked away, Grace saw Hades look back. Back to the woman he had once loved, to the woman he swore he would protect - and there was something new in his eyes - reverence.

Chapter Seventeen

Bride of the Underworld

✻

<u>Grace</u>

Grace stepped into the vast chamber, the sight before her caused her to falter for a moment. Smooth black obsidian formed an altar in the centre of the room, its polished surface reflecting the plumes of silver and pale yellow smoke that intertwined together. The scent in the air was filled with a fresh citrus, so sharp it made her skin tingle, excitement surging throughout her veins.

Hades stood by the altar, thick black robes hanging from his body like shadows, the edges shimmering with golden thread. Every step Grace took towards him made the crystal vibrate beneath her bare feet.

Her own milky white robe brushed against the floor, the curls of smoke winding around her body, highlighting the curve of her shoulders, the softness of her arms.

"Why the yellow smoke?" She asked Hades, her voice trembling slightly.

He moved closer to her, his vast frame towering. "The Fates have chosen it for you," he explained, voice deep and intimate, "A pale pastel lemon for you, Grace - the colour will become part of you - your skin will glow and shimmer as mine does. A subtle fire beneath the surface."

Grace's fingers brushed against the coolness of the altar, the hum surged at her touch, sending a shiver down her spine. "And this ... my immortality ... that happens now?"

Hades titled his head, his eyes trained on her, "If that is what you still wish."

"More than anything in this world - or the other one," she laughed, moving closer to Hades and allowing the electricity between them to guide her.

"Then let us begin," he whispered, extending a hand. The moment their fingers touched, a shot bolted through her, straight to her chest.

Everything about this moment - it just felt *right*.

The pull she had felt since entering the underworld - the one she had fought to ignore - hit her full force. It was overwhelming yet divine, like everything she had dreamed of.

Smoke pulsed around them in response, curling and blending in yellow-silver tones until it moved in shifting patterns across her skin. Grace felt pure heat and power flood her body, like a current running along every curve. Through the softness of her thighs, the swell of her hips, even igniting the faint stretch marks that lay hidden beneath her robe. She quivered under Hades' powerful gaze as he spoke in a tongue she could not understand.

"With this vow, I bind my soul to yours. Unfading, unyielding, unending." He whispered, a finite ending, bringing forth their eternal bond.

Humming light began to glimmer across Grace's skin, subtle at first, like a faint reflection on water. With each second, the swirls of lemon and silver became more intricate, touching every dimple and crevice until she glowed with undeniable beauty.

Hades' eyes widened, his usually unreadable face shone with joy as he took in her new appearance. "Grace ... I have never seen someone so beautiful in my entire life ... you are perfect."

She swallowed hard, everything about her felt different, and yet exactly right at the same time.

The immortality ritual was complete - she was no longer Grace, the mortal teacher from Derby - she was an ethereal goddess, Queen of the Underworld.

Before she could speak, Hades lifted her onto the altar, the icy coolness of the crystal contrasting the burning desire that flooded her veins. Her robe shifted slightly, falling from her shoulder and exposing a river of glistening skin, the light accentuating every contour of her body.

Then he kissed her.

First igniting a fiery trail down her collarbone, a teasing of lips that sent shocks down her spine. Grace fell against him, breath catching, every nerve in her body ignited.

"Say my name," he commanded, voice deep and filled with lust.

"Hades," she whispered, the word a surrender of her body - and a plea for more.

The room pulsed with heat as his mouth claimed hers, possessive and demanding. His strong hands slid beneath the thin muslin of her robe, cupping and exploring the delicate curves he had been craving. Fingers digging into smooth skin, grounding her in the moment, a feeling she never wanted to forget.

Grace flushed beneath his touch, every breath ragged. Her hands grasped at the front of his robes, exposing the hardness of his body - strong, real and beautiful. Hades travelled across the planes of her thighs, sliding higher, until the heat between them was unbearable.

Grace could not fight the feeling a moment longer, her fingers tangling in his dark hair, pulling him tight against her.

"Please," she begged, her voice desperate with desire.

Hades' eyes met hers, passion burned deep within him. There was no need to speak, he answered by entering her slowly, deliberately, giving her time to adjust to every inch, every movement.

The weight of him filled her, consuming and addictive. Raw power meeting willing surrender. She bit her lip, head thrown back to the ceiling, her nails dragging across his skin as he began to move - controlled and steady.

"Tell me again," he asked between rough kisses on her breast, "Tell me you're mine."

Grace could barely speak, the passion of the moment taking over, "I am yours. Always."

A possessive growl rumbled through Hades' body, and he brought her closer, driving his lust with increasing desperation, their bodies a fierce clash. Their sounds filled the chamber as Grace's body became alive with arousal, she arched her back, meeting him with equal fire.

And then the storm broke. Each shuddering wave of release crashed through her, raw and untamed. Hades held her close, whispering dark nothings against the bare skin of her neck. Trembling, Grace pressed a kiss to his throat, "I will be yours always," she promised, her voice husky with need.

And there, beneath the shimmering obsidian ceiling, deep in the heart of the underworld, a binding was sealed. Not just with power and ritual - but truth and desire.

Epilogue

A Sister Reborn

✸

<u>Fleur</u>

Fleur awoke to a quiet that was different - not really quiet at all. It wrapped around her like thick velvet, heavy and still, yet filled with unrecognisable whispers. She tried to move her body, but it would not co-operate, being *dead* did make things more difficult after all.

But then she saw her.

Grace. HER Grace!

Kneeling before her, radiant in a way that caused her chest to ache. Shimmering faintly, yellow smoke curled around her like sunshine in human form. Except - not exactly human - not anymore. Something was very different about her big sister.

"Fleur!" she exclaimed, voice steady but filled with excitement, "You're here! You're really here!"

Fleur opened her mouth, but no words came. Her eyes were drawn to the figure of her sister, the glitter of her skin, the way she carried herself with authority.

Grace reached for her hands tentatively, "I know this is ... a lot. But I will explain everything in time, I promise," She gestured to the man next to her, "This is Hades, we are sort of ... married. And we rule the underworld together."

Married??

To the Lord of the Dead? A man so terrifying his name struck fear into the hearts of every mortal on earth?

"I do not understand..." Fleur said, shrinking back slightly from the towering frame of a looming Hades.

"Try not to worry," he said, voice booming, "I promise there is nothing to fear - you will have only the best in our realm. It is what you deserve."

Grace smiled warmly at her *husband,* "And Hades is not as scary as he looks, I can assure you of that!"

Fleur swallowed hard, looking from Grace to Hades and back again. It was all so surreal. The sister she had known, soft and ... human, was gone. But the warmth in her eyes and the comfort in her smile remained the same.

And somehow that made the whole dying thing a lot easier.

"Welcome home Fleur, I have missed you," Grace said, placing a small kiss on the back of her little sister's hand.

And just like that Fleur realised.

Home wasn't a place, it was Grace.

It always had been.

Acknowledgments

Every book starts with a spark, but it takes a lot of people to turn that spark into a fire. I am endlessly grateful to the people who have helped me bring this story to life.

My wonderful BETA readers - Aimee, Leanne and Holly - thank you for your honest feedback, your unwavering support and your willingness to read this book even in its messiest stage!

A special thank you to Demi for being the most incredible friend, for reading random chapters of this book when I felt like giving up, for managing my ARC team and all round just being the BEST.

To all of my fabulous ARC readers and members of my book promotion team (Emma, Becky, Corie, Selena and Celeste) you have all been so encouraging, and I can not thank you enough for loving Mercy of Hades.

Bella - my cover designer - where can I even begin? You are pure magic! You captured this book's heart and soul, and I still cannot believe how lucky I am to work with you!

Big thanks to Megan and Keira for their wonderful character art! Seeing Grace and Hades come to life was amazing!

This book is a celebration of so many things. Of embracing softness and strength, of plus-size bodies taking centre stage, and of finding love in the most unexpected of places. I wanted this story to be a reminder to everyone - you deserve to be loved, seen, desired and chosen - not in spite of who you are, but *because* of it.

And finally, a brief mention of the Disney film '*Hercules*'. I fell for Hades long before I knew what that meant - the sass, the sarcasm, the whole chaotic villain energy. Turns out some crushes never really disappear, they just turn into full blown stories instead!

To you, the reader, thank you for reading, dreaming and falling for the villain right alongside me!

About the Author

Millie Bowker is independently published author of multi-genre romance novellas, with a passion for creating stories that celebrate love and diversity. Based in Staffordshire, UK, Millie is often found with her dog Sherlock by her side and an iced coffee in hand - no matter what the weather!

A firm believer in representation, she loves including chronically ill and disabled characters in her stories, alongside a strong focus on plus size positivity. Whether it's a historical series or a contemporary standalone, Millie's books strive to be a celebration of all kinds of love, bodies and experiences.

Always working on something new (usually too many projects!) Millie invites readers to escape into her worlds and discover unforgettable characters!

Millie loves to hear feedback from readers! Connect with her on social media!

Instagram - @millsandbooks **TikTok** - @millsandbooks_

Also by Millie Bowker

Regency Romance

<u>Unbound Hearts Series</u>

Book One - Healing the Wounded Earl

Book Two - Finding the Viscount's Son

(Coming February 2026)

Short Stories

Bloody Bunny (*Psychological Thriller*)

Printed in Dunstable, United Kingdom